FELIX

FEELS BETTER

ROSEMARY WELLS

At bedtime Felix ate
too many chocolate blimpies
and stayed up far too late.

274459

BETTER

First published 2001 by Walker Books Ltd
87 Vauxhall Walk, London SE11 5HJ

This edition published 2002

2 4 6 8 10 9 7 5 3 1

© 2001 Rosemary Wells

This book has been typeset in Veronan

Printed in Hong Kong

British Library Cataloguing in Publication Data: a catalogue record
for this book is available from the British Library

ISBN 0-7445-8926-6

WALKER BOOKS
AND SUBSIDIARIES
LONDON • BOSTON • SYDNEY

In the morning Felix's
mummy made pancakes.

"No, please,"
said Felix.

"You look peaky,
Felix," said
Felix's mummy.

"Let's get you toasty and
warm," she said.
Then Felix's mummy made
Felix a cup of camomile tea.

"Do you feel better yet?"
asked Felix's mummy.
"No," said Felix.
So his mummy gave him
some sugared prunes.

"You'll feel perkier
with the prunes," she said.

"Not
feeling
perkier,"
said Felix.

Felix's mummy
listened at the window.
Felix was not making
    his motorcycle noises.

"Something is wrong
with my Felix,"
she said.
So Felix's
mummy called
the doctor.

"Fresh air
will give
you a boost,"
said Felix's
mummy.

She bundled Felix
up and put him
outside on his
motorcycle.

"Bring him over
right away," said
Doctor Duck.

"Don't be afraid, my little moonbeam," said Felix's mummy.

But Felix was afraid.

Felix was
afraid the
doctor would
ask his mummy
to leave
the room.

But Doctor Duck
did not ask Felix's mummy
to leave the room.

Doctor Duck let
Felix's mummy stay with
him the whole time.

Doctor Duck listened
to Felix's heart.

Doctor Duck looked
in Felix's ears

and took his temperature.

Then he gave Felix two
spoonfuls of Happy Tummy and said,
"Call me in the morning."

Felix slept
all the way
home.

He didn't wake up
until he smelt
buttered toast and
lemon tea.

"Tomorrow let's go to the
circus and the cinema
and the funfair!"
said Felix.

"What about a picnic
in the canoe?"
said Felix's
mummy.

"We'll do it all!"
said Felix.